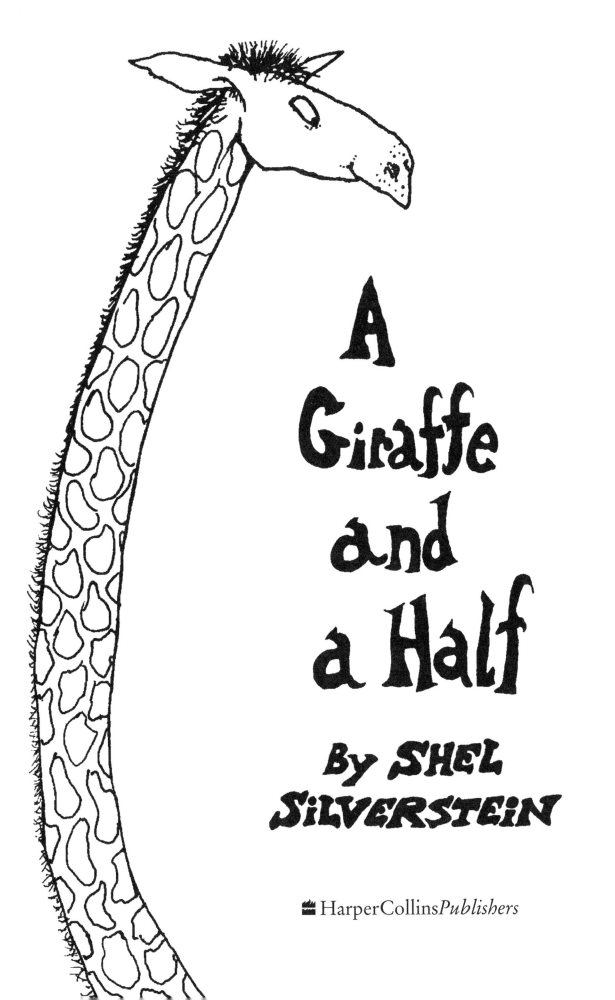

A Giraffe and a Half

By SHEL SILVERSTEIN

HarperCollins*Publishers*

A GIRAFFE AND A HALF
© 1964, renewed 1992 Evil Eye, LLC
The Shel Silverstein name and signature logo are trademarks of Evil Eye, LLC.
Printed in the United States of America. All rights reserved.
For information address HarperCollins Children's Books,
a division of HarperCollins Publishers, 10 East 53rd Street, New York, NY 10022.
Library of Congress Catalog Card number: 64-19709
ISBN 978-0-06-025655-5
ISBN 978-0-06-025656-2 (lib. bdg.)
13 14 15 16 17   LP/WOR   50 49 48 47 46 45 44 43

If you had a giraffe...

and he stretched

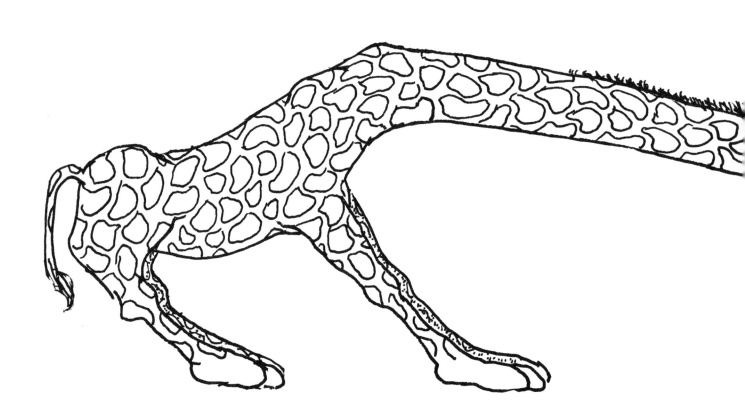

another half . . .

you would have

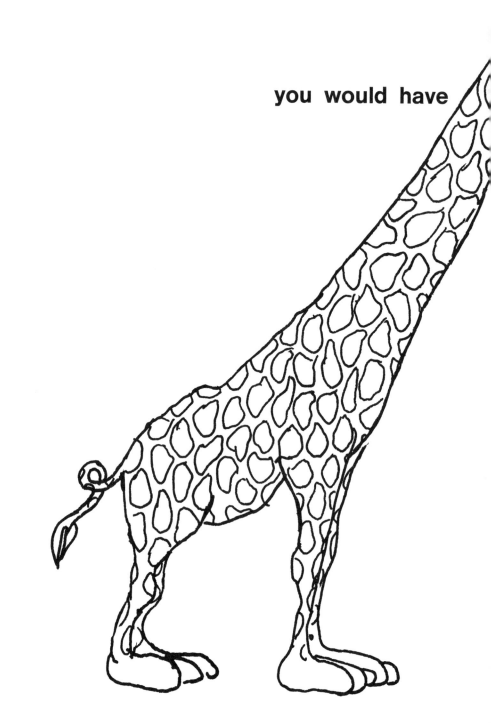

a giraffe and a half.

If he put on a hat
and inside lived a rat...

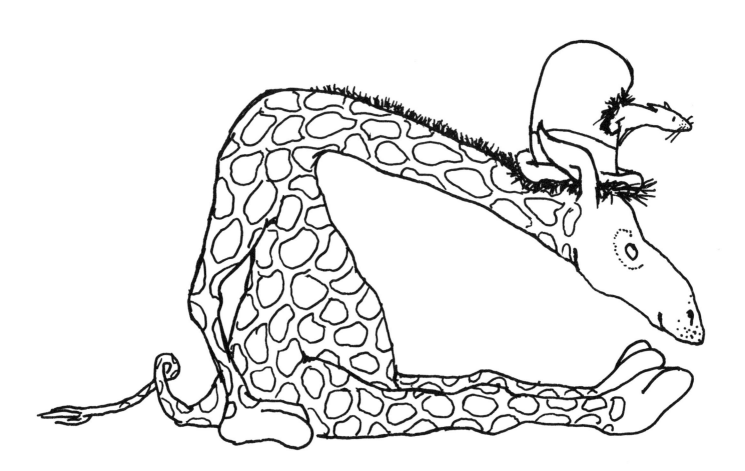

you would have a giraffe and a half
with a rat in his hat.

If you dressed him in a suit
and he looked very cute...

you would have a giraffe and a half
with a rat in his hat
looking cute in a suit.

**If you glued a rose
to the tip of his nose...**

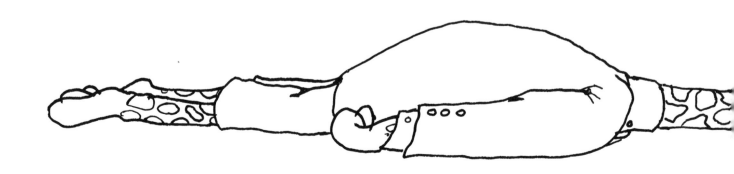

you would have a giraffe and a half
with a rat in his hat
looking cute in a suit
with a rose on his nose.

If a bumbley old bee
stung him right on the knee...

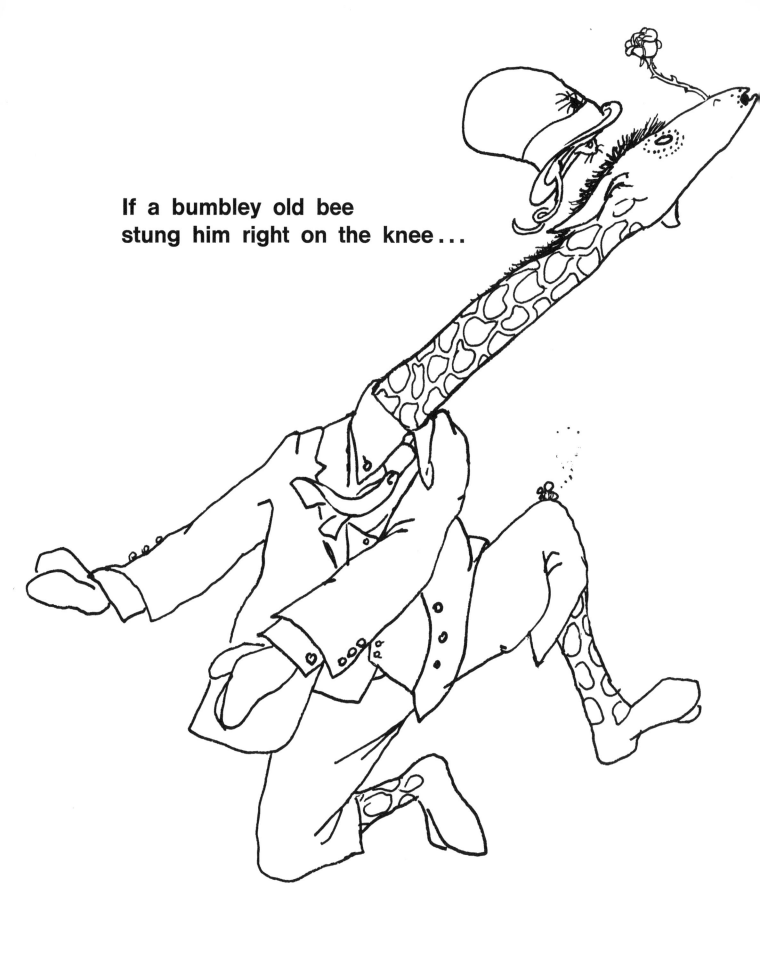

you would have a giraffe and a half
with a rat in his hat
looking cute in a suit
with a rose on his nose
and a bee on his knee.

If he put on a shoe
and then stepped in some glue...

you would have a giraffe and a half
with a rat in his hat
looking cute in a suit
with a rose on his nose
and a bee on his knee
and some glue on his shoe.

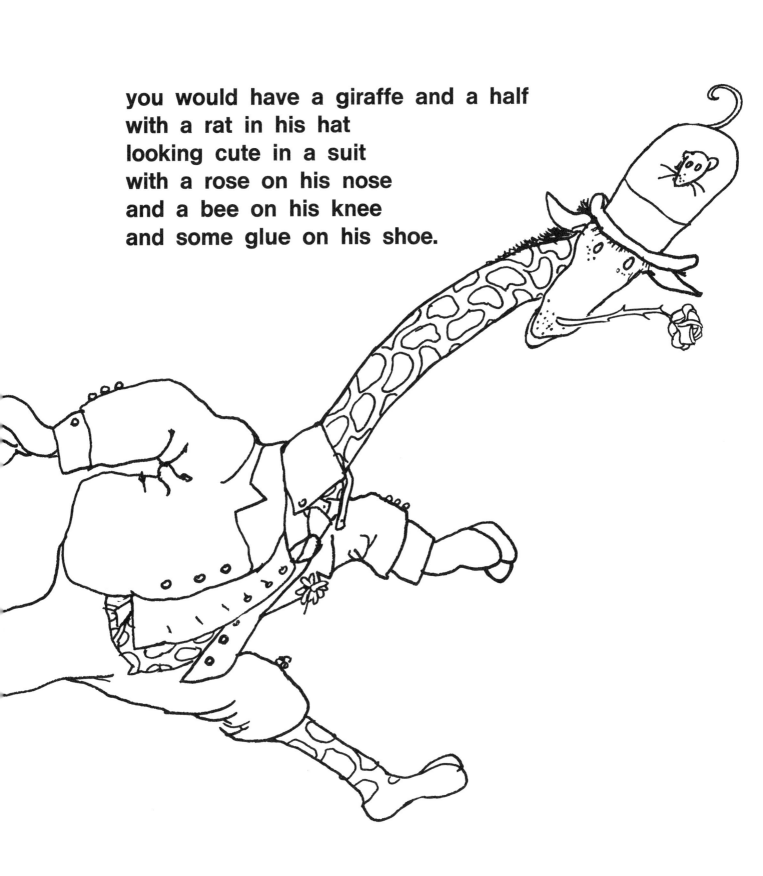

If you gave him a flute
and he played tooty-toot...

you would have a giraffe and a half
with a rat in his hat
looking cute in a suit
with a rose on his nose
and a bee on his knee
and some glue on his shoe
playing toot on a flute.

If he used a chair
to comb his hair...

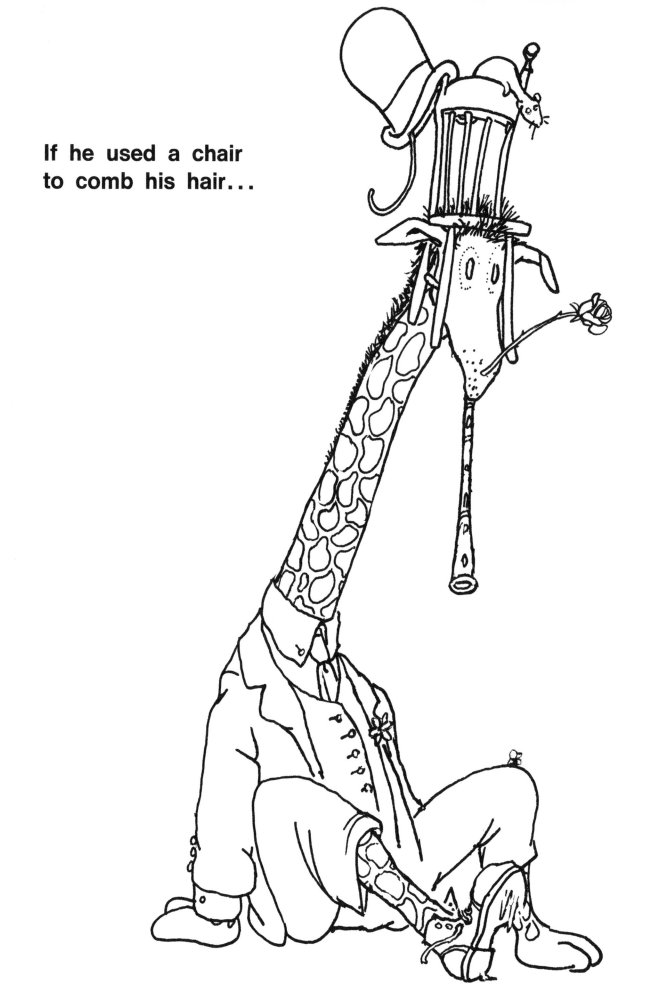

you would have a giraffe and a half
with a rat in his hat
looking cute in a suit
with a rose on his nose
and a bee on his knee
and some glue on his shoe
playing toot on a flute
with a chair in his hair.

If he tripped on a snake
who was eating some cake...

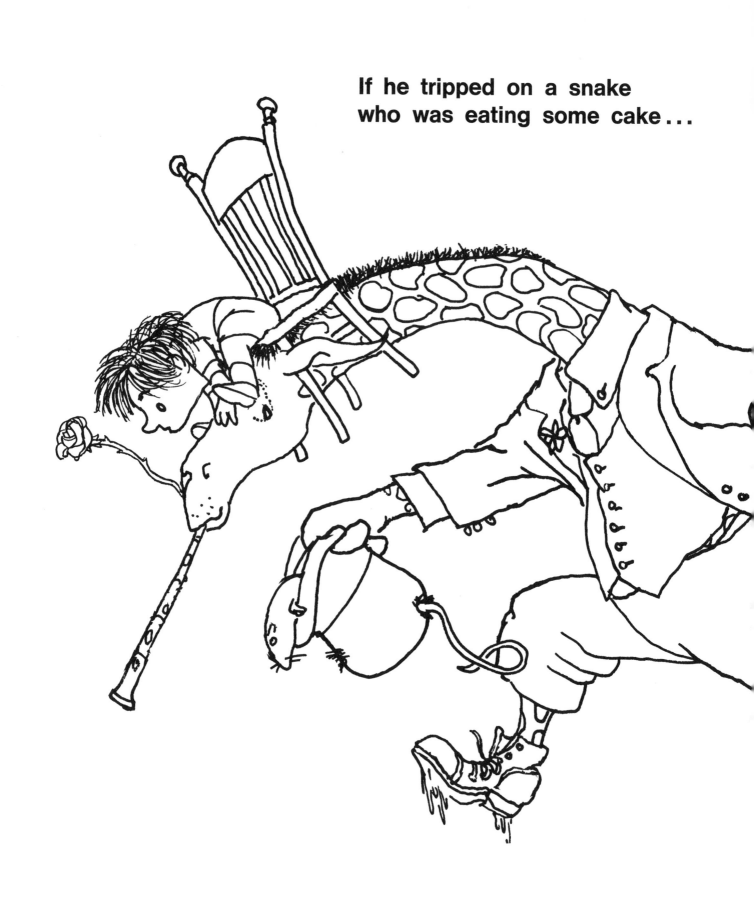

you would have a giraffe and a half
with a rat in his hat
looking cute in a suit
with a rose on his nose
and a bee on his knee
and some glue on his shoe
playing toot on a flute
with a chair in his hair
and a snake eating cake.

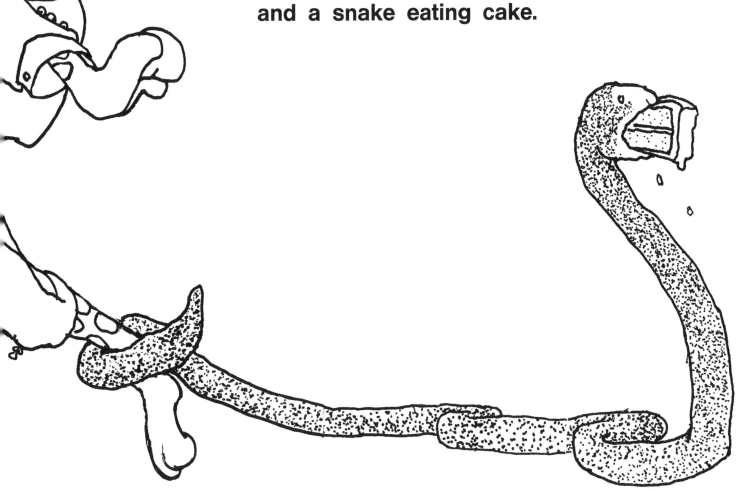

If he found an old trunk
and inside was a skunk...

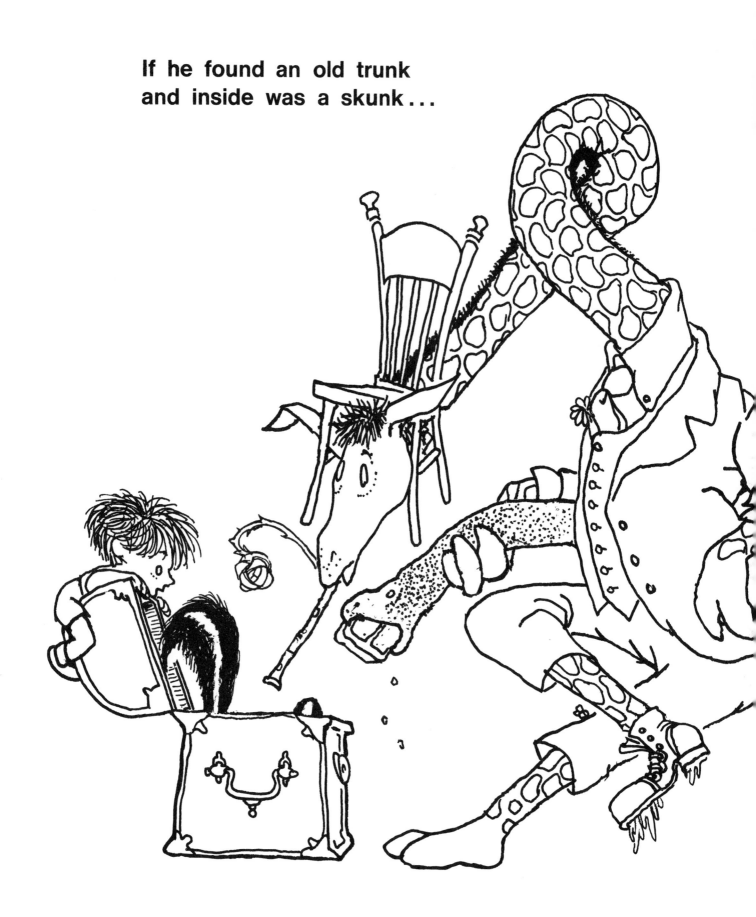

you would have a giraffe and a half
with a rat in his hat
looking cute in a suit
with a rose on his nose
and a bee on his knee
and some glue on his shoe
playing toot on a flute
with a chair in his hair
and a snake eating cake
and a skunk in a trunk.

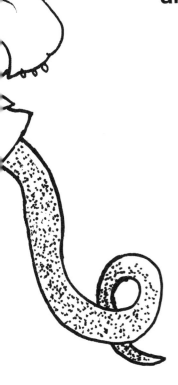

If he met a fat dragon
who sat in a wagon...

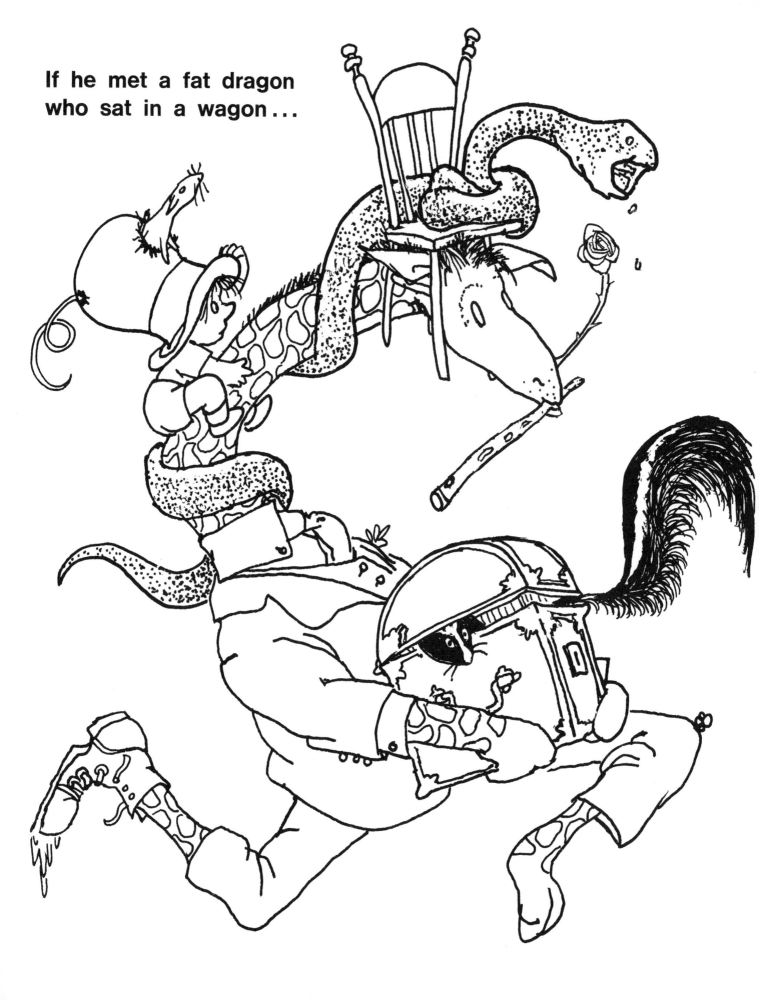

you would have a giraffe and a half
with a rat in his hat
looking cute in a suit
with a rose on his nose
and a bee on his knee
and some glue on his shoe
playing toot on a flute
with a chair in his hair
and a snake eating cake
and a skunk in a trunk
and a dragon in a wagon.

If he jumped on a bike
and rode over a spike...

you would have a giraffe and a half
with a rat in his hat
looking cute in a suit
with a rose on his nose
and a bee on his knee
and some glue on his shoe
playing toot on a flute
with a chair in his hair
and a snake eating cake
and a skunk in a trunk
and a dragon in a wagon
and a spike in his bike.

If a blubbery whale
got ahold of his tail...

you would have a giraffe and a half
with a rat in his hat
looking cute in a suit
with a rose on his nose
and a bee on his knee
and some glue on his shoe
playing toot on a flute
with a chair in his hair
and a snake eating cake
and a skunk in a trunk
and a dragon in a wagon
and a spike in his bike
and a whale on his tail.

If he fell in a hole
that was dug by a mole...

you would have a giraffe and a half
with a rat in his hat
looking cute in a suit
with a rose on his nose
and a bee on his knee
and some glue on his shoe
playing toot on a flute
with a chair in his hair
and a snake eating cake
and a skunk in a trunk
and a dragon in a wagon
and a spike in his bike
and a whale on his tail
in a hole with a mole.

But . . . if you brought him a pole
to climb out of the hole . . .

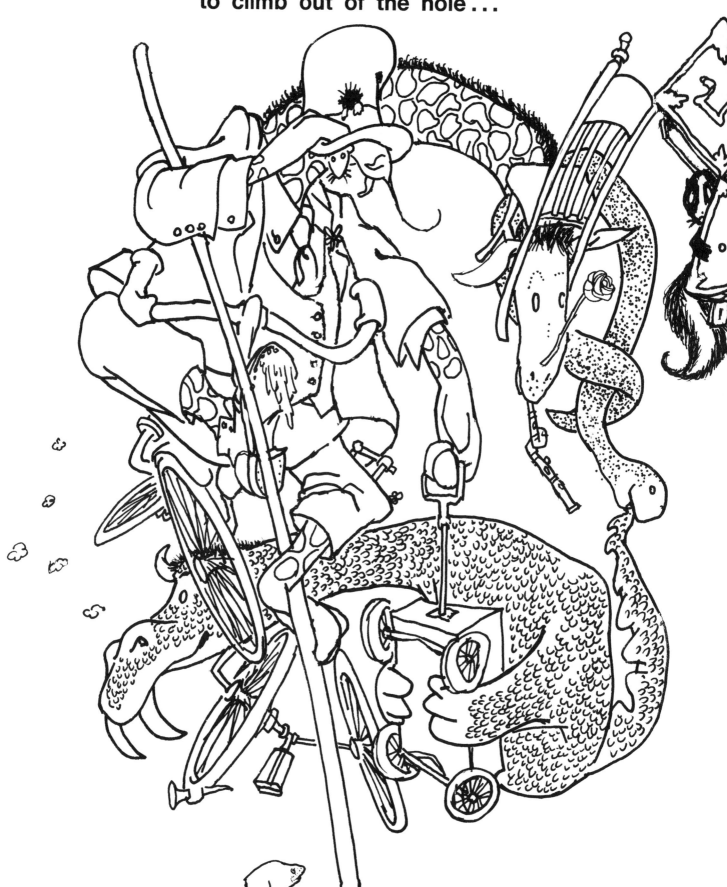

and the whale left his tail
and went off for the mail...

and he gave the spiked bike
to a scout on a hike...

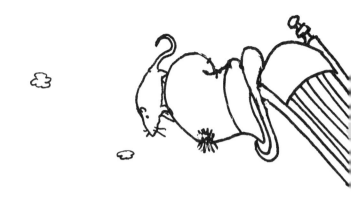

and he left the fat dragon
'cause his wagon was saggin'...

and he gave his chair
to a tired old bear...

and he traded the flute
to a bird for some fruit . . .

and he told that old snake
to go jump in the lake...

and a man who bought junk
bought the trunk with the skunk...

and he gave the rose
to a girl he chose...

while the bee on his knee
flew away with a flea...

and he put the shoe
with the glue
on *you* . . .

and that silly old rat
ran away with his hat...

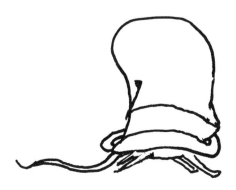

**and he put his suit
in the laundry chute...**

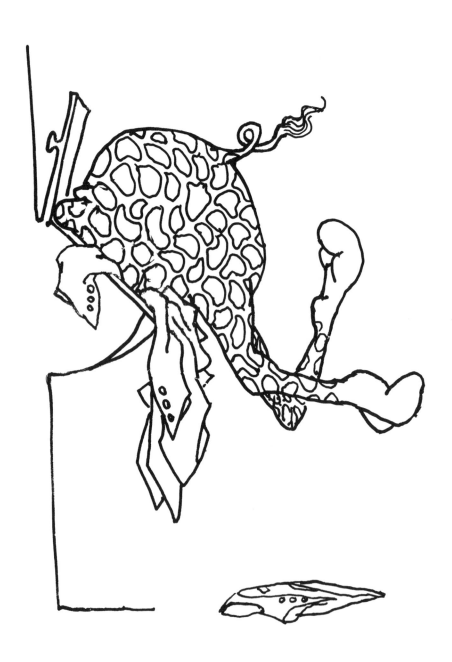

and he shrank another half...

you would have a giraffe!